LEGO® STAR WARS®

THE YODA CHRONICLES TRILOGY

BY ACE LANDERS
BASED ON THE SCREENPLAY BY MICHAEL PRICE

SCHOLASTIC INC.

Scholastic Children's Books,
Euston House, 24 Eversholt Street,
London NW1 1DB, UK

A division of Scholastic Ltd
London ~ New York ~ Toronto ~ Sydney ~ Auckland
Mexico City ~ New Delhi ~ Hong Kong

This book was first published in the US in 2014 by Scholastic Inc.

Published in the UK by Scholastic Ltd, 2014

ISBN 978 1407 14259 3

Printed and bound by L.E.G.O., Italy

2 4 6 8 10 9 7 5 3 1

PART I
ATTACK OF THE CLONE

It was a time of peril as the Clone Wars raged on with no end in sight.

But the Sith, led by the sinister ***DARTH SIDIOUS***, *had concocted a plan that could bring about the downfall of the Republic.*

The evil General Grievous flew directly towards Coruscant, home to the famous Jedi Temple Academy where Padawans trained in the ways of the Force. "I have the target in sight," Grievous said gruffly. There was an ominous plan underway.

Meanwhile, at the Jedi Temple Academy, Master Yoda instructed his Padawans using the Holocron. "The skills of a famous Jedi – who a Padawan like you, once was – you will see," said the ancient Jedi Master.

Yoda engaged the Holocron and the dome filled with holograms of Anakin Skywalker fighting fierce droidekas with his lightsaber.

But then a deeply troubled look came over Yoda's face as he detected a growing danger from the dark side. "A disturbance, I feel in the Force. A new threat, I detect; very powerful, this feeling is."

Yoda decided to contact Chancellor Palpatine and the news was not good. Palpatine claimed that he had received a distress call from Obi-Wan Kenobi. Obi-Wan was under attack on Alderaan, and it was up to Yoda to rescue him at once.

However, unknown to Yoda, Palpatine and Darth Sidious were the same person, and this was the beginning of a new wicked plan to destroy the Jedi Order.

The Padawans begged to help their teacher, but Yoda knew the mission would be too dangerous. Instead, he left C-3PO in charge as the substitute teacher. And as Yoda ran out, he Force-pushed a big textbook labeled INTRODUCTION TO JEDI POWERS to C-3PO and yelled, "The odd-numbered problems on page forty-six, do! All work, show!"

To run his rescue mission, Yoda needed some of his best fighters. Luckily, R2-D2, Clone Commander Cody, and Mace Windu answered the call. "I'm with you, bro!" said Cody.

"Wait," said Mace, "all of us Jedi have to call you 'Master,' but he gets to use 'bro'?"

"How I roll, that is." Yoda shrugged.

OUTIE, WE ARE!

As Yoda and his team left Coruscant, General Grievous landed and sneaked into the Jedi Temple. He found exactly what he was looking for inside the Holocron vault.

The Padawans wanted to fight, but knew they were in trouble when Grievous drew four lightsabers out from under his cloak. Finally, the Padawans put their hands up. Their powered-down lightsabers clattered to the floor.

IN MY CAPACITY AS ACTING TEACHER, WE SURRENDER.

Meanwhile, Yoda arrived at Alderaan and called for Obi-Wan Kenobi. But Obi-Wan had never called for help. He was on vacation!

"A mystery, this is," said Yoda. But then the mystery was solved when a fleet of Separatist ships surrounded them.

"It's a trap!" gasped Yoda.

"Well, duh," cackled Captain Ackbar, the pilot of Yoda's ship.

The Separatist ships opened fire on Yoda and his crew. Their Republic gunship blasted back, but the Jedi were seriously outnumbered.

"Retreat to Coruscant, we must," ordered Yoda.

Captain Ackbar tried to make the jump to lightspeed, but the ship rumbled and broke in two. The bottom section with Yoda, Mace, and R2 was left floating in space.

GETS BETTER AND BETTER, THIS DAY DOES.

With the Padawans cornered, Grievous collected their lightsabers and hid them under his cloak. "Don't worry, these will be put to good use ... by the Sith!"

The Padawans couldn't let Grievous steal their special weapons! They attacked the cyborg, kicking, punching, and poking him as he made his escape.

"Don't poke my eyes!" screamed Grievous. "They're my only real things!"

Finally, shaking like a wet dog, Grievous flung the Padawans off his back and blasted off in his ship.

VROOOOOM

"Well, that's that," said C-3PO. "Nothing we can do now. At least he only took your lightsabers."

But the Padawans were determined to get their weapons back, so they boarded their school-bus ship against C-3PO's commands. The substitute teacher droid followed them onto the ship in an attempt to stop their rash behaviour, but faster than a speeding parsec, the Padawans lifted off and blasted after General Grievous.

Yoda, Mace, and R2 plummeted out of the sky and landed in a murky swamp with a giant splash. Pieces of their broken ship fell all around them. Floating in the lagoon, Mace said, "I guess we're somewhere called Dagobah."

LIKE THIS PLACE, I DO. LIVE HERE SOMEDAY, I COULD.

Later by the fire, Yoda and Mace struggled to figure out who had betrayed them. "Could Master Plo Koon be the Sith Lord?" asked Mace.

"Him? Never. Kit Fisto?" suggested Yoda.

"How about Mas Amedda?" asked Mace.

"Not sure who that even is, I am," admitted Yoda.

"Blue guy? Two big horns?" explained Mace. "Works for Chancellor Palpatine." Just then the two Jedi shared an inspired look.

"Chancellor Palpatine!" they echoed. "We can ask him who he thinks the Sith Lord is!"

Elsewhere, the Padawans used their Jedi skills to locate their lost lightsabers far away on the desert planet Tatooine.

"And just how do you plan on getting halfway across the galaxy in a bus?" asked C-3PO.

"I've made a few modifications," said Bene. "Engaging hyperdrive engines."

Suddenly, vents on the side of the bus opened and two huge engines popped out. Then Bene yanked the throttle and the ship zoomed into hyperspace, sending C-3PO crashing against the back of the bus.

JEDI TEMPLE
SCHOOL DISTRICT

Once on Tatooine, the Padawans were drawn to Mos Espa. There they found Watto, a junk dealer, who had purchased their lightsabers from Grievous. However, Watto had already sold the lightsabers ... to the creepy crime boss, Jabba the Hutt.

"That slimy slug has our lightsabers!" said Bobby.

"And we're going to get them back," said Rako.

"I was afraid you would say that," C-3PO worried out loud.

That evening, C-3PO walked up to Jabba's palace and nervously knocked on the door while the Padawans hid behind a rock.

Reading from a cue card, C-3PO said, "Jabba the Hutt is a big stupid jerk who smells like the inside of a tauntaun!"

The door flew open revealing an angry Bib Fortuna, Malakili, and the rancor who took off chasing the slender droid.

RAWRRRR!

YOUR PLAN IS WORKING PERFECTLYYYYY!

With the coast clear, the Padawans sneaked inside and found Jabba snoozing, and holding their lightsabers like a teddy bear. They gently retrieved the lightsabers, until Bobby accidentally stomped on Jabba's tail and woke the slumbering super villain.

Jabba's scream alerted his Gamorrean guards, who rushed in with weapons drawn. "Hold it! You kids are rancor food."

"That's what you think," said Rako as the Padawans wielded their lightsabers once again. But nothing happened. The lightsabers wouldn't turn on.

"The crystals are gone!" shrieked Bene.

"Get 'em!" said the guards.

The guards chased the Padawans, but then the rancor returned, with C-3PO holding onto its back for dear life. "This isn't nearly as much fun as it looks!" he hollered.

"Hang on, Threepio, I'll help you," said Vaash Ti. She used a Jedi mind trick to calm the furious beast. "You are a good boy," she said.

Instantly, the rancor became as gentle as a cute, little puppy; then the Padawans climbed onto the monster's back and rode away.

Meanwhile, Yoda and Mace were still stranded on Dagobah, when a mysterious ship hovered about them. "Hands up, trespassers! This is a restricted planet. You have some nerve coming here!"

The Jedi drew their lightsabers, ready for battle, but then a mystery figure descended from the spaceship with a big smile. "Just kidding – I got your distress call! The name's Calrissian – Lindo Calrissian. And this is my son, Lando. And this is the *Millennium Falcon*. Need a lift?"

Once on board, Yoda was contacted by C-3PO about his Tatooine adventure.

"Threepio-See, why go to Tatooine, did you?" asked Yoda.

But Bobby explained, "A coughing robot took our lightsabers so we had to get 'em back from the worm-guy's house, but somebody stole-ded the crystals so now they don't work!"

Yoda and Mace knew instantly that Grievous was working with Count Dooku and that the lightsaber crystals could be used to create Sith clones. "To Kamino, we must go at once!"

As the rain fell on Kamino, Count Dooku and Grievous contacted Darth Sidious to confirm they had the kaiburr crystals from the Padawans' lightsabers. Grievous handed over the four small crystals and Dooku assembled them into one giant, glowing piece.

"And now we are ready to create your new weapons, my master," said Count Dooku as they entered a room filled with sleeping Sith clones waiting in clone chambers.

But as the clone chambers pulsated with a blinding light from the kaiburr crystals, Yoda and Mace charged in with their lightsabers drawn.

"Fast, so not, Dooku!" cried Yoda. "Failed, your evil plot has."

Grievous attacked, rapidly swiveling his lightsabers until they cut the floor into a trapdoor and the cyborg fell through it. Then Mace and Yoda used the Force to knock Dooku against the clone centre's power source, dislodging the kaiburr crystal.

ENDED, YOUR EVIL QUEST IS, DOOKU,

But then a light pulsated from underneath the battle debris. With a great explosion, a single chamber opened and one clone stepped out.

I AM READY TO FIGHT

FOR THE SITH!

Then the Sith clone raised his arm and shot an intense blast of Force lightning at Yoda, Mace, and R2. "You have done well, my creation, but I have more of you to make. Rebuild my cloning room," commanded Dooku.

With an amazing display of Force-building powers, the Sith clone, JEK-14, reassembled the ruined cloning facility brick by brick. Yoda and Mace knew they needed to stop more dangerous Sith clones from being created. They charged at JEK, but he blasted them with Force lightning again.

SKKKKK

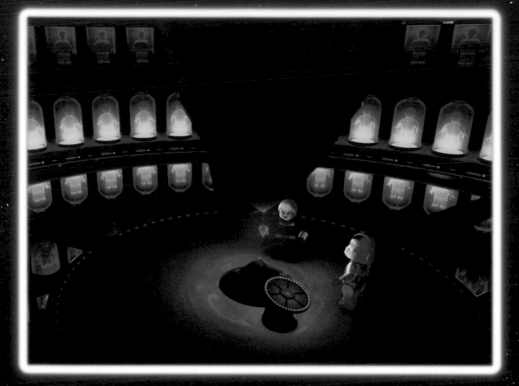

Meanwhile, Dooku put the crystal back in its podium. The crystal started to glow and its energy flowed back to the cloning chambers. Yoda attempted to retrieve the power source, Force-pushing Grievous into Dooku and knocking them both flat. JEK did not miss a beat.

The clone blasted another beam at Yoda, but this time Yoda dodged the attack.

Mace, however, was hit and thrust out into the Kaminoan rain on to a landing platform.

Grievous advanced on the wounded Mace with his robot arms stretching out from underneath his cloak. But in the rain, the cyborg slowed to a halt. "My joints! They're rusting in the rain!"

"Should have paid extra for the undercoating package," yelled Mace as he picked up his lightsaber and ran back to help Yoda fight JEK.

COULD SOMEONE GET ME AN OILCAN?

Suddenly, the entire wall of the cloning facility exploded open with one of JEK's beams that hurled Yoda out on to the platform.

"My Sith clone army is almost complete! Now, finish them," Count Dooku commanded.

Before JEK could unleash a final blast on Yoda and Mace, C-3PO and the Padawans arrived in their bus.

"*Ooh*, a bus full of children. I'm terrified," laughed Dooku.

Giant laser cannons popped out from underneath the bus and blasted a hole in the dome of the cloning facility. The entire building began to collapse as C-3PO grabbed Yoda and Mace.

"The crystal!" yelled Yoda. "Still in the cloning room, it is."

"Not anymore!" said C-3PO. "Look!"

R2 flew out from the crumbling rubble with the kaiburr crystal. Yoda and the Padawans had defeated the Sith's evil plan.

"Saved the Republic, you Padawans did," cheered Yoda. "Proud of you, I am."

"But, Master Yoda, the Sith clone survived," said Rako.

"And dangerous, he is," admitted Yoda. "But find him, I will. A promise, that is."

Back on Geonosis, Count Dooku stood before Darth Sidious. "Lord Sidious, allow me to present our most powerful new weapon."

"Sith clone JEK at your command, Master," said the clone who pulsated with the dark side of the Force.

Darth Sidious smiled a crooked, mean smile. "Excellent. You and I are going to lay waste to the galaxy together."

PART II
REVENGE OF THE JEDI

WAR!

Now that I have your attention . . .
The dreaded DARTH SIDIOUS has
summoned his forces to Geonosis
to unveil a secret weapon that will

ensure ultimate victory for the

Sith. There is bumper-to-bumper

excitement.

The Sith and Separatist leaders came from all around to hear the evil news. Asajj Ventress, Darth Maul, Count Dooku, General Grievous, and more piled into the Geonosian arena to hear their leader speak.

Finally when everyone was settled, Darth Sidious began his speech. "Comrades in evil ... I'd *like* to tell you that we are winning this war."

"YAY!" applauded the crowd.

"But I can't," Sidious continued, "because we're losing!"

"BOO!" groaned the crowd.

"But, starting today, things are going to change," promised Sidious. "The Jedi and their ilk have outsmarted us for the last time!"

Hiding within the crowd of the galaxy's worst villains, a cleverly disguised Obi-Wan and Yoda were waiting to discover Sidious's next big plan.

"Victory will be ours," the Sith Lord continued, "now that we have created the Ultimate Weapon … JEK-14!" The Sith clone stepped out onto the balcony beside Sidious, but the crowd did not applaud.

"That's your ultimate weapon? A clone?" asked Nute Gunray. "You guys seem a little desperate."

"And you seem a little fried," said Sidious as he pummeled Nute with Force lightning. "JEK – show 'em what you got!"

JEK lifted his glowing left arm into the air and shot out an awesome stream of Force lightning. Then he leapt from the balcony and flipped around the arena, firing bolts of lightning everywhere. As the exploded bricks rained down, JEK used the Force to form the debris into a special message for the nonbelievers: GO SITH!

Elsewhere, the Jedi Council faced a decision destined to have grave implications for the Republic. C-3PO no longer wanted to serve as substitute teacher to the Padawans. Luckily, the Jedi Council had already found the perfect substitute for the substitute while Master Yoda was away on his special mission.

I CAN'T BELIEVE THEY STUCK ME WITH THIS STUPID BABYSITTING JOB!

"What would Obi-Wan say?!" complained Anakin Skywalker to R2-D2 as he drove the Padawan bus.

The restless Padawans were on a field trip of discovery and contemplation to a planet which had played a crucial role in Jedi history.

"Told you," groaned Rako. "It's Hoth."

"C'mon, Hoth is great!" said Anakin with fake enthusiasm. "It's a little chilly, but it's exciting. I love it!"

YOU'RE A GREAT JEDI –
BUT YOU'RE **NOT** A VERY
GOOD ACTOR.

JEK continued his display of power back on Geonosis, tearing apart battle droids and droidekas, then recombining them into a gigantic mega-battle droid and then obliterating the behemoth in one shot.

"A bad feeling about this, I have," said Yoda.

There was only one JEK now, but Sidious and Count Dooku had perfected the art of Instant Clone-Cloning of Clones. They would use JEK's power to create an army of Sith clones!

Strangely, when JEK entered the clone machine, his power was quickly drained. And when he came out, he was very weak. "JEK will regain his strength," assured Count Dooku. "So we can make an army of exact replicas of him, just like ... this one!"

As the second door opened in a cloud of smoke, an exact mini-clone of JEK stepped out!

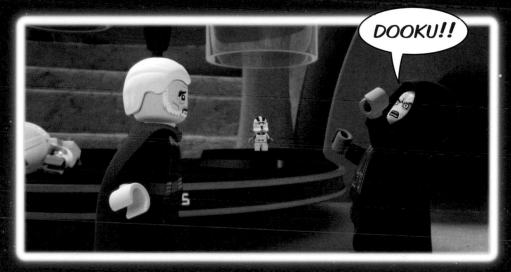

DOOKU!!

Having seen enough, Yoda and Obi-Wan threw off their disguises and attacked the entire arena full of bad guys!

"Jedi Knights?!" Darth Sidious shouted. "Bad guys, do your stuff!"

Sidious stood aside as his minions tried to battle Yoda and Obi-Wan. First Obi-Wan pushed Grievous into Asajj Ventress, knocking them both out. Then Yoda used the Force to pull Count Dooku's cloak over his eyes. Then Mini-JEK attacked Yoda, but Yoda flicked him away like a tiny bug. Darth Maul stepped forward next, but with a gentle nudge of Obi-Wan's finger, the Sith

NOT COOL!

Lord tipped off his robot legs, which ran around in circles. Only Sidious was left, but instead of fighting, he escaped in a spaceship.

"Well, that wasn't too hard," said Obi-Wan who was suddenly struck by a massive bolt of lightning. They had forgotten about JEK.

BAM!

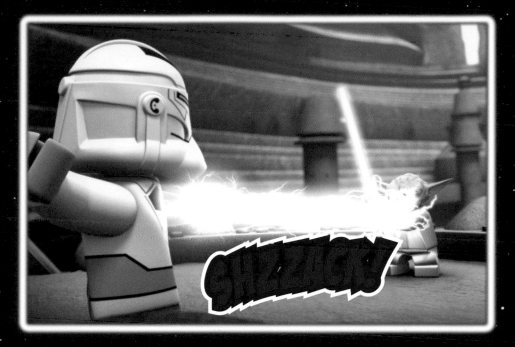

SHZZACK!

Having regained the upper hand, the Sith fell upon the Jedi. Asajj and Grievous sparked a vicious lightsaber duel with Obi-Wan while Yoda dodged JEK's barrage of bolt blasts. Finally, JEK landed a shot and slammed Yoda into a column, knocking the Jedi's lightsaber away. "Victory is ours!" cried Dooku. "JEK – finish him."

"But, Master—" the clone halted. "He's unarmed."

"Made from a Jedi crystal, you were," said Yoda. "The Force runs through you. Choose the light side, you still can."

FWOOOSH

Clearly torn between the light side and the dark side, JEK announced, "I choose ... *neither* of you! I want to be me!" Then, turning his arm into a shield, JEK sent out a massive Force push that knocked everyone down and allowed him to escape in a ship.

Yoda and Obi-Wan swiftly followed him, with the villains chasing him as well. But JEK lost them all in a torrent of evasive flight manoeuvres before blasting away into hyperspace.

Meanwhile on Hoth, the wind and snow whipped fiercely around the cave Anakin and the Padawans had made their base. Anakin reached out to C-3PO for some teaching advice, but instead he learned that all was not well in the galaxy.

"Oh, it's quite hectic indeed," said C-3PO, "what with the escaped Sith clone and the galaxy-wide search for him going on. Master Yoda has even resorted to hiring bounty hunters."

Back in the Jedi Temple, the room was filled with the most bloodthirsty, notorious bounty hunters ever assembled. Obi-Wan and Yoda observed the crew from the corner.

"Do we really need these unsavoury fellows?" asked Obi-Wan.

"Crucial, finding this clone is," confided Yoda. "And not with Jedi alone can we do that. Lucky we are that refuse to work for the Sith these bounty hunters do."

And so both Sith and Jedi launched a massive search – scouring every corner of the galaxy for the Sith clone, JEK-14.

On Hoth, Anakin sighed as a pair of probe droids flew past in the sky. The Padawans sat around him in a circle with their textbooks on their laps. "Every other Jedi is looking for that clone, and I'm stuck here with a bunch of kids," said Anakin. But while Anakin was complaining, the Padawans detected something in the Force. The young ones quietly slipped out of the cave as Anakin continued his whining.

"They think I'm not ready, but I am. I'm not a child anymore. I'm going to bring balance to the Force. I can do anything!"

HEY, WHERE'D EVERYONE GO?

Not far from the cave on Hoth, the Padawans discovered JEK. He was busy building beautiful things from the surrounding bricks.

"For being part Sith, you're so gentle," said Vaash Ti.

"I don't want to fight," said JEK. "I just want to create things and be left alone."

"Something tells me you're not going to get your wish," said Vaash Ti as Anakin charged JEK with his lightsaber drawn. But JEK was protected in a Force bubble and Anakin merely bounced away.

BOING!

Suddenly, JEK was attacked from all directions by the probe droids. His ship was disintegrated and his limp body fell through the air. "No!" the Padawans screamed. They did not want to see the gentle clone harmed. Before hitting the ground, JEK landed on top of General Grievous's starfighter. "Got him!" the cyborg exclaimed as he pulled the unconscious clone into the ship and zoomed away.

Grievous brought JEK back to the Separatist ship where Count Dooku's clone machine was waiting.

"You've failed me as a warrior," Dooku said to JEK, "but don't worry – I can still use you to make millions of clones." Then Dooku placed the groggy and helpless JEK into the cloning pod and shut the door. Grievous started the clone machine and, as the destroyer made its way to Coruscant, new Sith clones came to life.

YES! COME TO LIFE, MY CLONED CLONES!

Knowing that the Sith clones were coming to destroy them, the Jedi Council met to discuss the best way to handle the attack.

Obi-Wan chided Anakin's hologram. "Your conduct was rash and irresponsible. Anakin, stay put. Don't do something foolish like rush back here and join the battle to make up for your mistake."

Anakin paused with a guilty look on his face. "Uh … I guess you could say that ship already sailed."

In the Padawan bus, Anakin swerved to avoid the blast from the Separatist destroyer that lurked just outside of Coruscant. Activating the cannons, Anakin returned fire. Meanwhile, the Council watched the battle below.

"Defend the Temple, we must!" announced Yoda. The Jedi sprang into action.

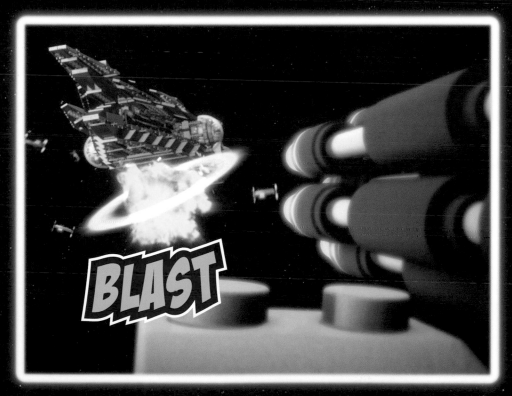

BLAST

But they were too late. Clone after clone after clone spilled out from the clone machine, as Count Dooku cackled maniacally. "Yes, yes! Now we will see what an entire army of Sith clones can do!"

JEK remained in the host pod, very weakened and straining to stay alive. The clone machine was using up all of his power.

As the battle raged on in space, the passengers of the Padawan bus found themselves in the middle of all the excitement. Anakin and R2 looked for a way to defeat the destroyer, but couldn't find one. Then their ship was hit and started to fall apart!

Anakin had an idea. "Padawans, we're not done yet. Remember JEK ... and create!" As the bus began to break apart, they used the bricks to Force-build spaceships for each of them.

"I never thought I'd say this ... but you actually taught me something!" said Raku.

GREAT IDEA, ANAKIN!

Anakin flew around the command ship looking for a weak spot, but he couldn't find it. While he was distracted, Asajj Ventress lowered her ship into position. She was about to destroy the Jedi

BSSSSHTKSST

when her ship was rocked by laser fire! It was Bobby the Padawan in his Force-built spaceship. "You are not a nice lady!" he said, firing on her ship and saving Anakin.

Landing on the command ship, Anakin found the weak spot. He used his lightsaber to puncture the hull, and was blown out to space where the Padawans rescued him. They watched from a safe distance as the ship exploded. The enemy vessel and its terrified crew plummeted towards the Jedi Temple.

BOOOM!

On the temple's landing pad, Anakin and the Padawans joined Yoda and the other Jedi to watch the destroyer's bridge tumble into the atmosphere.

"Great work, Anakin," said Obi-Wan.

"Yes! Victory is ours!" spat out Chancellor Palpatine sarcastically. *"Go, Jedi! Go, Jedi! It's your birthday, it's your birthday!"*

But, taking a step behind the others so he couldn't be seen, Palpatine used the Force to help the Sith ship stay together and land safely.

Count Dooku stumbled out and yelled, "Okay, Jedi – surrender or die!"

"We will fight you to the death, Dooku!" said Obi-Wan. "Now give us that clone."

"Delighted to," said Dooku as he tossed the lifeless JEK onto the ground. "You see, I don't need him ... because now I have all of THEM!"

CLONED CLONES, ATTACK!

An army of cloned clones marched out onto the platform and stood ready to attack. Slowly, each raised his crystal arm and took aim at the Jedi. With a mighty zap, the cloned clones fired a concentrated Force-beam.

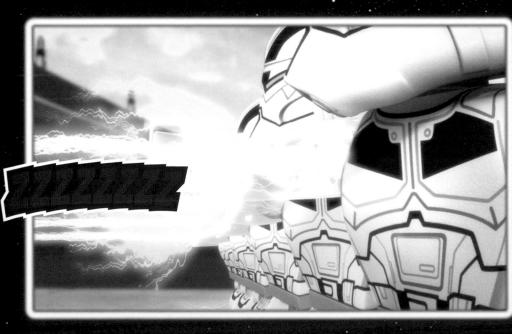

ZZZZZZZ

But before the blast hit its mark, another powerful Force-beam erupted and stopped the cloned clones' strike.

It was JEK! "Not with *my* energy you don't."

The Padawans cheered on as JEK used every ounce of his strength to gather up all of the cloned clones, creating a giant ball of energy that surged back into himself. The cloned clone army became useless mini-clones and JEK's full power had returned. He forced the mini-clones into space and turned his attention back to Dooku.

HEY! WHAT'S GOING ON? WHO SHRUNK US?

"I thought I told you to LEAVE ME ALONE!" screamed JEK as he sent out one last blast that lifted Dooku and Grievous off into space.

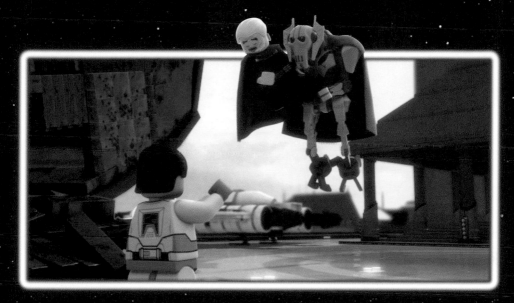

Yoda stepped forward and began to speak, but JEK interrupted him. "That goes for you, too. I like you all, but I have to go my own way. Please don't call." And with that, he jetted away in his spaceship.

Later, Yoda, Obi-Wan, Anakin, and the Padawans revisited the JEK adventure through the Holocron.

"Long remembered in the chronicles of the Jedi, will your exploits in this battle be, my Padawans," said Yoda. "Proud of you, am I."

PART III
THE BADAWAN FINISH

The tide of the war has turned.
DARTH SIDIOUS's plot to create
an army of SITH CLONES has
failed, along with his other plot
to clone the one CLONE the SITH
did clone into CLONES cloned
from that CLONE. I have no idea
what I am saying. . . .

Let's just say the bad guys are
losing.

Back in the heat of battle, Anakin Skywalker and Obi-Wan Kenobi found themselves in the Geonosis desert parrying blasts from Separatist battle droids.

An X-wing flown by C-3PO and R2-D2 zoomed overhead, blasting Asajj Ventress and Darth Maul below.

General Grievous and Count Dooku were watching over the battle from afar. They knew that Separatist reinforcements were coming and that there was nothing to fear. That is until the new batch of battle droids arrived, saw that the Jedi had blown apart their other troops and ran the other way. Without backup, Dooku and Grievous took the same cue and retreated on foot.

Yoda zipped in on a Republic ship and called out, "Fleeing, they are! After them!" He suddenly fell out of the ship.

But the Padawan bus swooped in to the rescue. Yoda landed on top of the bus, straddling the laser cannon.

"We've got you, Yoda!" said Bene.

The Padawan bus landed safely and Yoda climbed off to meet with Obi-Wan, Anakin, R2 and C-3PO. The enemy had fled.

"Master Yoda," said Anakin, "Geonosis is ours. Do you know what this means?"

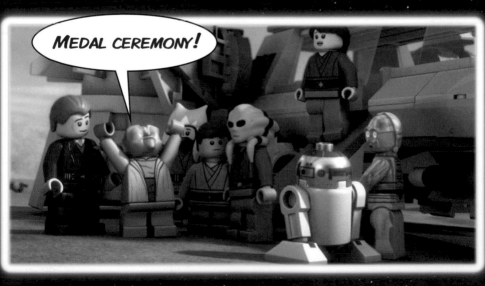

MEDAL CEREMONY!

Back in Coruscant, Chancellor Palpatine was addressing the Senate, pretending to revel in the Jedi's victory. "And, so, as your Supreme Chancellor ... I am overjoyed to report that – once again – the Sith have been defeated by, essentially, four children, two droids, and an 800-year old green guy."

The Senate let out an uproarious cheer.

On the lava planet Mustafar, Count Dooku and others had gathered to regroup after their latest loss. "We Sith have a new strategy. It's not clones that we need ... but more apprentices." Then, gesturing to his right, Dooku proudly announced, "We have officially rescinded 'The Rule of Two,' and I am happy to welcome you as our first Badawans. We, your teachers, hope you are *Bad* enough to succeed."

A group of several young Badawans listened to their teacher. When Dooku was done, one raised his hand. "Uh, Count Dooku, right? You know your name sounds like *doo-doo*, right?" The Badawans all began to laugh, until Darth Maul drew his double-bladed lightsaber and demanded that they show their teachers some respect.

"Sorry," said a Badawan girl. "By the way, do you know what time it is?"

"Sure," answered Darth Maul, but when he turned his wrist to check his watch, one half of his double-bladed lightsaber dipped into the lava river.

"Time for you to get a new lightsaber," she giggled.

WHY, YOU LITTLE—*!!*

Commander Cody was on a recon mission and happened to be spying on Count Dooku. "All the baddies in one place," he said to himself. "Commander Cody to Obi-Wan Kenodi. I' ve got news that'll blow your mind, bro."

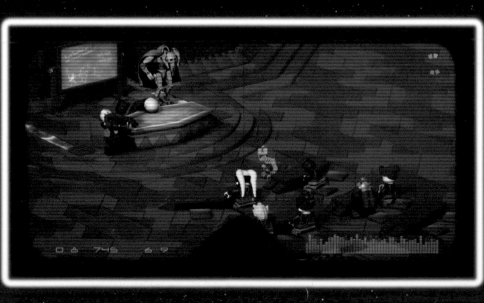

Meanwhile, the Republic Senate was motioning for an all out "We Won the War" party, but Palpatine could barely hide his discomfort. "Now, now, hold on. I want to win as much as the next Supreme Chancellor, but let's not be hasty. The war is far from over."

"Not so fast, Chancellor!" said Obi-Wan as he and Anakin zoomed in on a Senate platform. "We've just learned that several major Sith Lords and their new apprentices are gathered together on Mustafar."

WIPE OUT THE ENEMY, WE COULD, WITH A SURPRISE ATTACK!

Anakin agreed, "Every available Jedi is on their way to prepare for the attack now, Master."

"Then it's time to victory-party down!" cheered Lindo Calrissian as he hit a button and a disco ball descended from the ceiling and music blared.

As the other senators partied, a grim Palpatine disappeared out of sight.

Alone in his Senate Chamber, Palpatine pulled on his hood and became the evil Darth Sidious. He called Count Dooku immediately. "The Jedi are planning a surprise attack. But they'll be surprised when we ambush them! It's my favorite thing ... a trap! Will the Badawans be ready?"

"Uh ... yes, yes! Of course!" answered Dooku nervously.

"They don't look so ready to me," groaned Sidious as he watched Darth Maul scurrying around trying to catch his own legs.

"They are a handful," admitted Dooku.

Sidious studied the Badawans as they continued to act badly. "Alright, I'm coming there to whip those Badawans into shape and personally lead the ambush."

As Palpatine jumped in his shuttle, he was confused to see the landing pad crowded with Jedi and clone troopers.

"Massing our fleet for the attack, we are," said Yoda to the shocked Chancellor. "Going where, are you?"

"Uh, I want to ..." Palpatine paused. "Come along with you, and ... watch our great victory! Yeah, that's it."

The Jedi agreed to allow Palpatine to join them, but under one condition: he had to travel with Obi-Wan and Anakin for protection. C-3PO would even serve as his protocol droid.

Back at the Sith Academy, Count Dooku paced back and forth in front of the Badawans. They squirmed nervously in their seats.

"Yes, you better be scared," Dooku smiled. "Because Darth Sidious, the evilest man ever, is coming to teach you some manners ... now!"

But Darth Sidious did not arrive and the Badawans began to snicker silently.

"Just you wait!" snapped Dooku before sending Grievous to find their boss.

THE BIG MAN WILL BE HERE REEEEAAALLY SOOOOOOON...

LORD SIDIOUS!
IT'S ME!

As the Republic fleet was about to set a course for Mustafar, General Grievous's ship pulled up right alongside Palpatine's shuttle. Grievous waved and smiled. "It's me – Grievous! I WORK FOR YOU!"

Palpatine screamed out, "He's-lying-I-don't-know-him-I've-never-met-him-I'm-a-good-guy!"

"He must be trying to assassinate you," hollered Anakin.

"That's ridiculous," started Palpatine before changing his mind.

I MEAN, YES!
ATTACK!

Once Grievous saw that Obi-Wan and Anakin were on Sidious's shuttle, he turned to escape, but found himself face-to-face with the entire Republic fleet. Quickly, Grievous hightailed it into an asteroid field, but the Jedi followed him. Grievous manoeuvred his way out of the asteroid maze without getting blasted by the Jedi and made the jump into hyperspace.

Yoda commanded the fleet to jump into hyperspace after Grievous to keep him from ruining their surprise attack. However, Yoda did not account for where the other ships in the fleet were aiming. The entire fleet crashed into each other at lightspeed.

"An oopsie, I made," whimpered Yoda just before an explosion sent bricks flying everywhere.

BOOOOMMM

Yoda crawled out from under a pile of bricks. They had all crashed into an asteroid that was now covered with bricks.

"Blew this, I did," said Yoda. "Now ruined, the entire fleet is."

"Not all of it," said Rako as he gestured to the freshly rebuilt Padawan bus.

The Jedi Master was astonished. "Do that so fast, how did you?"

Palpatine bounded over, full of energy and excitement. "Excellent work! Now we just need someone to take the bus to Coruscant and get some new ships. How 'bout me?"

"Time, we have not. Warn the Sith, General Grievous will, I fear. Need our fleet repaired now, we do."

"Master Yoda, we know someone nearby who can help us put all our ships back together quickly," suggested Bene.

"Impossible!" cried Anakin. "All of the Jedi are here."

"He's not exactly a Jedi." Bene smiled.

The Padawans, Yoda, C-3PO, and Palpatine all blasted off to Endor, where the Sith clone JEK had been hiding.

"Hi, JEK!" said the Padawans happily.

"Oh, come on – you again?!" said JEK. "I told you the last time to leave me alone. I'm not a Jedi, and I'm not a Sith. The answer is no. I won't help you."

But the Padawans turned on their winning charm and convinced JEK with their irresistible smiles.

"Okay, I'll fix your ships," sighed JEK. "But that's it."

But the Jedi's efforts were too late. General Grievous was able to contact Count Dooku and warn him that the Republic fleet was on its way to attack.

And worse than that, they were coming with Palpatine/Sidious in tow!

"Then get back here," demanded Dooku. "We must prepare."

"Um … I think I'll just keep looking for Lord Sidious," said Grievous as he could see the madness the Badawans were creating at the academy.

Back on the asteroid, the brick mess stretched for miles and miles.

"Wow. Some mess you've got here," marvelled JEK.

"Yeah, well, good luck putting a dozen ships back together, genius," said Anakin.

JEK simply made a quick gesture with his glowing arm and, instantaneously, all the scattered bricks came together into one huge, new megaship.

"I – I don't believe it," Anakin gasped.

"That ... is why you fail," said JEK.

"Use that line some day, can I?" asked Yoda, who was very impressed.

To ensure the Chancellor's safety, Yoda had asked Palpatine to remain behind on Endor with C-3PO, far, far away from the epic battle which could potentially destroy the Sith forever.

Surrounded by dancing Ewoks, Palpatine had an idea for how to escape. He began coughing. "Oh, no! Ewok dander! My throat is closing up – I must get away from here!"

Then he rushed over to JEK's ship and blasted off to lead the Sith to victory as Darth Sidious.

"Hope you feel better!" cried C-3PO. "Imagine, being allergic to Ewoks."

Sidious zipped along in JEK's ship, imagining his new life after he defeats the Jedi. "I shall rule the galaxy as  president. No, wait – king! No – emperor! I like the way that rolls out. 'Emperor Palpatine' ... super evil."

But then General Grievous spotted the ship. "It's that ungrateful Sith clone!" fumed Grievous, assuming JEK was inside. Grievous fired a missile. "Die, Sith clone!"

UH-OH.

As JEK put the finishing touches on the megaship, the Jedi, Padawans, and clone troopers all climbed aboard.

SAVED US, YOU DID.

AND GRATEFUL, WE ARE.

"Don't mention it," said JEK. "Good luck with your battle."

"Need it, we will," admitted Yoda. And with that, the Republic fleet set off again for Mustafar to finish the battle.

General Grievous's ship entered the atmosphere of Mustafar and headed for the lava river below. Riding alongside him was a very angry Darth Sidious.

"How could I know it was you?!" asked Grievous innocently. "I'm not a mind reader."

"If you were, you'd know I'm ticked at you right now!" chided Darth Sidious. "But I'm in a forgiving mood since this will be my happiest day ever. Once again, the Sith will rule the galaxy!

Darth Sidious entered the Sith Academy to find all of his teachers trapped by the Badawans. "Stop this nonsense at once!" he commanded as he zapped the Badawans into place. "We have no time to lose. The Jedi fleet will be here soon and we will be waiting to ambush them!" But then there was a loud hum overhead. Sidious looked up to see that the Republic's megaship had already arrived.

"Chancellor, why talking to Sith Lords are you?" asked Yoda.

"Um ..." stalled Palpatine. "I was giving them a chance to surrender. But they won't, so attack!"

A huge battle erupted! A massive army of droidekas rolled out and started firing at the megaship. Yoda, Obi-Wan, and Anakin leapt out to take on Dooku, Ventress, and Darth Maul in lightsaber duels. The Padawans zipped down ropes and drew their lightsabers against the Badawans.

Meanwhile, Palpatine used his leadership role to confuse the Republic clones and lead them into Sith traps. In no time, the Republic was outnumbered and retreated out onto a few rocks surrounded by lava. There was no escape.

ZZAKTTT

Suddenly, as the Jedi had their backs against the wall, a bolt of Force lightning blasted away the entire encroaching Sith army. The Padawans looked up to see JEK hovering above them. "It's JEK! He came back to help!"

"I can't help it, I like you guys too much," said JEK. But then he saw Count Dooku trying to sneak away. "But you almost destroyed me!" He fried the Sith Lord to a crisp with Force lightning and turned to Yoda. "I think you should leave now."

"Tell me twice, you don't have to."

The Jedi, Padawans, and clone troopers quickly got back on their megaship. "Wait for your loyal leader!" cried Palpatine as he ran up the ramp last.

JEK turned to the cowering Sith. "Here's one thing you should remember: Being. Bad. Is. Not. Good!" With each word, he blasted at the bad guys. The last blast hit the Sith command centre, exploding it to pieces.

Back at the Jedi Temple, the Republic celebrated their victory and cheered for JEK as he shot his own fireworks into the night sky. Everyone in the Republic rejoiced – that is, except for Chancellor Palpatine and a solemn Anakin.

"Something wrong, Anakin?" asked Palpatine.

"Why should that clone get all the glory? I'm the Chosen One!"

"Indeed," agreed Palpatine. "Well, *I* think you're a great Jedi."

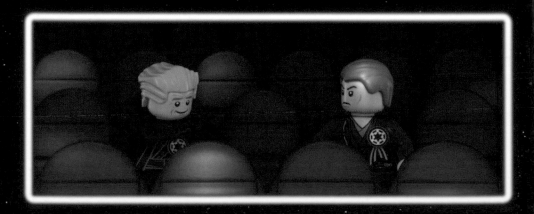